W9-ALK-144

WARM AT HOME

BY **RONI SCHOTTER**

ILLUSTRATED BY **DARA GOLDMAN**

MACMILLAN PUBLISHING COMPANY   NEW YORK
MAXWELL MACMILLAN CANADA   TORONTO
MAXWELL MACMILLAN INTERNATIONAL   NEW YORK   OXFORD   SINGAPORE   SYDNEY

Text copyright © 1993 by Roni Schotter. Illustrations copyright © 1993 by Dara Goldman. All rights reserved. No part of this book may be reproduced or transmitted in any form or by any means, electronic or mechanical, including photocopying, recording, or by any information storage and retrieval system, without permission in writing from the Publisher. Macmillan Publishing Company is part of the Maxwell Communication Group of Companies. Macmillan Publishing Company, 866 Third Avenue, New York, NY 10022. Maxwell Macmillan Canada, Inc., 1200 Eglinton Avenue East, Suite 200, Don Mills, Ontario M3C 3N1. First edition. Printed in the United States of America. The text of this book is set in 14pt Icone Light. The illustrations are rendered in colored pencil.
10 9 8 7 6 5 4 3 2 1

Library of Congress Cataloging–in–Publication Data. Schotter, Roni. Warm at home / by Roni Schotter ; illustrated by Dara Goldman. — 1st ed.   p.   cm.   Summary: Home sick with a cold, Bunny plays with or eats everything in his room. ISBN 0-02-781295-2 [1. Rabbits — Fiction. 2. Cold (Disease) — Fiction. 3. Play — Fiction.] I. Goldman, Dara, ill. II. Title. PZ7.S3765War   1993   [E] — dc20   91-48145

For Iris and Wendy — *sisters*!
"We'll build our house and chop our wood and make our garden grow."
— R.S.

To my daughter Sarah, with love
— D.G.

Bunny was sick. His nose twitched and his eyes were wet and swollen the way they got when he'd eaten too many onions.

"You can't go out today," Mama Rabbit said. "It's raining. You must stay warm at home until you are well."

Bunny hated those words. When his mother wasn't looking, he snuck to the door of the rabbit hole and poked his head out. Outside in the wide, wonderful world, the sky look as sad as Bunny did. It rained down fat, wet tears on everything.

"But there's *nothing* to do inside," Bunny complained. "Cabbage-cabbage-cabbage-*chooo!*" he sneezed at his mother and crept into his room.

"Nothing to do," he said out loud to himself because that was all he could think of doing.

He grabbed two shiny teaspoons he'd found in the garden. Tapping them together, he beat out a rhythm. "Nothing to do," he sang out.

"Nothing to do," he said, marching.

"Nothing but nothing but NOTHING to do!" he said, tripping over his rug.

Bunny rested for a while on the floor, tangled in his carpet. Then he picked himself up and hopped to his window boxes to water his plants. How tasty they would be one day if only he could leave them alone and let them grow!

"But I'm sick," Bunny explained to the plants. "And there's nothing to do. Leekity-leekity-*chooo!*" He sneezed to prove it. "Maybe a tiny taste of cress would cheer me up." So he nibbled the curly tops off the cress in one window box; then, unable to stop himself, he ate the stems.

Pretty soon, there was no more cress, only the sign that showed where the cress had been. "Parsnipity-snippity-snippity-*snip,*" Bunny sniffled contentedly.

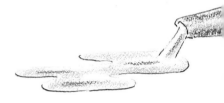

Bunny looked around his room. In the corner he spotted his rock collection. Bunny chose his biggest, flattest rock. Then he found the next biggest one and set it on top. Soon he had built a tower. Bunny climbed up the tower and posed like a statue on top.

"Give me your lettuce," he called out. "Give me your leeks! Give me your radishes, turnips and beets. I shall eat all day!"

The base of the tower wobbled, and the statue crashed to the floor.

Being a statue and thinking about all those vegetables made Bunny hungry again. He hopped to a window box and yanked at the top of a plant. Out popped a tiny baby carrot. "Sweeeeet," Bunny crooned when he'd swallowed the carrot, top and all. He pulled up another, then another....Before long, he'd eaten all his carrots.

Bunny lay down and pressed his fat belly against the floor. Flattening himself out, he could see under his bed where it was dark and damp. In the corner were some old acorns, a bunch of twigs, and a round, hard turnip.

Bunny grabbed the turnip and leaped happily to his feet. "Play ball!" he shouted. He propped his pillow against the wall and took his position.

"It's Bunny on the mound," he announced, tossing a few practice balls at the pillow. He needed to perfect his rabbit ball. He concentrated on trying to get as much hop into it as possible.

"Here's the windup," Bunny called. "Here comes the pitch...and it's...str-rike one." Bunny waited a moment or two, scratched his stomach, and pitched again. "Strike two!" he called out. Then, "Strike three, and Bunny strikes him out!"

He was hungry all over again and thought he deserved a
reward, so he ate the ball.

"Woody, but good," Bunny said contentedly. "Only now the
game's over and there's...*nothing to do.*"

Bunny lay down on his bed. He closed his eyes and pictured all
the things he could be doing outside if only he weren't sick.

"Chicory-chicory-chicory-*chooo!*" Bunny sneezed,
remembering the fine feeling of wind on his fur.

That gave him another idea. He hopped to a window box and
pulled a beet out of the soil. He nibbled and scraped it with his
teeth until he had shaped a colored pencil, just right for drawing.
Then he found a piece of paper he'd been saving.

Settling comfortably on the floor, he drew a picture of the world outside and all the things he loved in it, big and beautiful, runny and red, the color of beets. Then he drew another picture, of the world *inside*, and all the things he loved in *it*.

When he finished the drawings, he felt proud, so he ate the pencil. It tasted so fine that he ate the rest of the beets in his window box, trying as hard as he could not to stain his fur and the floor. "Messy, but delicious," he said. "Only now there's nothing to do *and*" — he checked his empty window boxes — "nothing to eat!"

Bunny looked at his drawing of the world outside and then he had his *most* wonderful idea. He pushed two chairs into the center of his room, draped his blankets across them, and made a tent. He grabbed his pillow and a book and crawled inside.

"Starry, starry night," he whispered, peeking out of the tent and pretending his ceiling was the night sky.

Bunny kicked at the inside of the tent. *"Whooooosh!"* he blew, pretending he was the wind. *"Swooooosh!"* he howled. "Too cold to go outside!" So he snuggled up, cozy and warm in his tent, to read until the weather cleared.

When the wind died down, Bunny crawled out to gather twigs.
Piling them carefully in front of his tent, he placed his wastebasket
on top, and pretended he'd built a campfire.

He'd eaten all his *real* vegetables, so he pretended some celery and onions. He put them in the kettle and added some imaginary parsley for seasoning. Then he stirred the mixture with a twig.

"When it's cold and windy out, there's nothing like vegetable stew," Bunny said. He closed his eyes tight and pictured the

vegetables softening up in the kettle. He imagined the sharp flavor
of the onion as it combined with the watery juice of the celery.

It was lunchtime now. Bunny was very, very hungry. He
thought about stew. He concentrated on stew. It seemed as if he
could actually smell stew.

He inhaled deeply and, when he opened his eyes, it wasn't a dream. Mama Rabbit was standing in front of him carrying a large platter, and sitting on the platter, right in the center of it, was a glass of carrot juice, a plate of plum crumble, and a large, steaming bowl of...vegetable stew!

"Lunchtime." His mother smiled.

"Oh, Mama!" Bunny felt warm inside.

"Bunny," Mama Rabbit said, her eyes widening as she looked around his messy room. "What did you *do* this morning?"

"Plenty," Bunny said proudly. "Plumitty-plumitty—" Bunny
nearly sneezed, but didn't. His cold was better! Maybe if it wasn't
raining tomorrow, he could go out, or maybe he would stay warm
at home, and...replant his window boxes!

Hmmm, he thought. A patch of peas might be nice. Some parsley, leeks, and lettuce. Bunny took an extra-large gulp of carrot juice. He needed energy. Tomorrow was going to be a busy day!